E
PO

Poulet, Virginia

Blue Bug and the
bullies

skip

hop

hang

slide

roll

crawl

climb

dig

hide

stand

BOO!

THE END
(Of the bullies)

The BULLIES

ant

cricket

 water bug

 daddy longlegs

wasp

dragonfly

beetle

centipede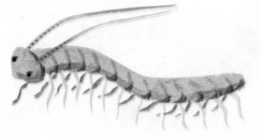

ant lion

spider

praying mantis

Blue bug could. Could you?

run	roll
jump	crawl
skip	climb
hop	dig
hang	hide
slide	stand